RISE A HAUNT

JACK KELLY

DEDICATION

To those who were there in those dark days

ACKNOWLEDGMENTS

Thank you Google Search and the Internet for all the assists. To first readers ADW and Kate for the comments and suggestions. The APE book written by Guy Kawasaki and Shawn Welch was a big help on this adventure too.

AUTHOR'S NOTES

The City of New Orleans is both the setting and a character in this story. No effort to accuracy was attempted in measuring distance, or direction, or time to move between any two points. Any faults are strictly the authors. Thank you.

blur

A phone rings in a darkened house at an hour which can only be described as ungodly. It screams against the single hour of sleep which its owner has managed to grab in what feels like a week and a half. This may or may not be a true assessment of the time period given. No one can really say anymore, minus the ordinary hum of a city alive and marching under the ordinary constraints of clock and calendar. The occupant has mostly lost the ability to mind the track of time of late and the lack of sleep has not helped. Nor has the absence of electricity, which has only recently been fleetingly restored, causing all of the hours of the day to scramble all together, with one falling into the other at seemingly random intervals. Day becomes night and night becomes day. The indifferent sun rises and falls as it always has in permanent contrast to the intervals of both moon and stars blinking even here, above the in-between.

Throw in the occasional clouded day over the city and it has become harder to tell Thursday from Tuesday. Still the phone screams for attention and the occupant finds himself wishing to be almost anyone else and any place else than who he is and where he currently finds himself. Only a far recess in his brain even notes the strangeness of a phone ringing, a sure sign of service and if he picks up the phone, of a connection made however fleeting. This thought is so far back in his brain it doesn't feel remarkable at all when his hand reaches out from the bed stretching for the phone, but unable to quite reach it, unless he were to also shift his body to extend the reach of both hand and arm. This is something his body seems particularly loathe to do in this particular moment of time. A moment he'll look back on fondly much later. He'll recall it as almost peaceful compared to the moments which will follow, even if it too will become lost in the countless hours and days that roll into one single *blur.*

those eyes

The description is always the same. Start with a tall, thin, very pale person, or perhaps wan creature, dressed in black. Undoubtedly female, but god, where did the strength come from? Those eyes too, eyes that will haunt a person forever. At least that is, when there's a description to be had. When anyone was found who was willing to bear witness especially after a glimpse into *those eyes.* The victims are never found in a condition lending itself to them being able to speak for themselves, let alone identify their attacker. An attacker who so far has been leaving behind no leads or any real evidence of any shape or form, let alone anything from which to even hazard a guess, to provide any answer to a question or conduct anything like an investigation. There are rumors and there are 'eyewitnesses.' Most of the victims were, before each one's untimely demise that is, victimizers themselves; or at least, in the act of death, involved in a matter of criminality. This connecting factor makes most leery of interrupting the process, putting all speech to law and order aside in the moment. Besides, the details, if known to the general public, would speak to an almost freakish nature of the crimes. The dead, to a person, have all died by an act they themselves had initiated or by a practice they'd previously had something more than a novice understanding of. They have all died almost by their own hand.

The victim tonight is a perfect example with his hands around the hilt of his own knife. A knife it was said he'd had a predilection for though probably not of this nature. The knife is buried deep in and through his own abdomen. It's driven with such force to have severed his spine before pinning him to the brick wall which he now rests against, one foot taller than he'd been in life. That is, he's raised almost a foot off of the ground from where he'd been standing when he'd been stabbed.

Funny ironic that - never thought the word 'stabbed' could have so little meaning as to be unable to describe how they'd found this guy. The cops always hated the freaky ones. And they'd all been freaky ones, every last one of them. There have been so many of these freaky ones currently, that the numbers to the crimes have lost any meaning and fall instead into a different category. It was the last, and the most fitting category, left for these events to fall into. It's not by plan mind you, it's by pure happenstance. In a year or more when these events have slipped from the public consciousness, all that will be left is the little dusty and hopefully soon to be lost in the bowels of bureaucracy, file collectively known as the "gruesome statistic."

something like bliss

A man stumbles along the street looking half drunk or in some kind of stupor. Neither circumstance is all that strange an occurrence here in this city. It's so naturally common that neither she nor anyone else notices the man, but there's this oddness to his stumble speaking of something else. He lurches along in a way she knows she's seen before, even if she couldn't place it, as the saying goes, to save her life. Suddenly the image comes to her even if it's still in its original black and white glory like she'd seen it the first time. It's Cagney, James Cagney in some gangster movie she can never remember the name of. It's near the end of the movie. Cagney's dying as he too stumbles through a different version of city streets with snow falling. Then, like in the movie, the man stumbles up a small flight of stairs leading to a church. The difference here is this is an abandoned church deep off the Quarter, somewhere lost in The Marigny. He disappears from view as he falls against the doors and they give way with his weight.

She's curious enough to follow him inside the church. A tick of the clock and she finds him sprawled out against the cold stones of this very old place with his face down and an arm bent beneath him. This man is obviously not your ordinary drunk as evidenced, if nothing else, by the noticeable cost and cut of his clothes. Finally, the gunshot wounds dotting his torso mark him as well as atypical.

All she can keep thinking, even as she flips him over onto his back, is how she shouldn't care and wouldn't care in any other circumstances. But then there's the damn movie running through her head and she sees Cagney fall again and again against those damn steps. She'd rather leave like she'd never been here at all, but it's too late for it. Because no one, for whatever reason, deserves to die alone and death's coming for this man, she's certain of it. She can recognize it now even with a side wards glance, as she and death have become more than passingly familiar with one another of late.

He's still alive, much to her surprise, given the wounds she's noticed and cataloged. He's also in excruciating pain. She leans down pulling his arms across his chest in the classic funeral position.

He's fighting for breath and for voice, something that's always amazed her when she's witnessed it. Still startling that people who are so close to death seem to suddenly want to speak so much, to have so much to say for themselves. She leans into him placing one hand on his crossed arms and one on his forehead and whispers to him, but it doesn't seem to comfort him. Her presence instead agitates him causing him an even greater urgency to find voice to whatever it is that troubles him and trembles upon his lips.

"Shush," she says to him again and then is lost within herself in a search to push her presence into him.

It's not the struggle one might imagine, there's little he can do to resist given his current situation, especially with both her and death so close. She leans in close and brushes her lips in a small pucker against his, allowing her weight to rest fully upon him. The kiss floods his body and his pain is taken into her person like sustenance. His previously ragged breathing steadies, as his heartbeat slows now that it's no longer locked in a struggle it cannot win.

Peace descends upon him understanding maybe, though compliance is a better term. It's not for her to know as he slips beneath the veil and passes over to the other side. His countenance shifts in those last moments as resolution to events sinks into the deepest parts of his person for a moment. It's a very brief moment when there's something like bliss passing through him. A word passes his lips which would be too shallow to hear for any who are not, like she is, lying upon him. The word is rapture, and she counts them both as blessed as only she can, because at least, with whatever small comfort she hopefully provided, he will not be stuck as she is in the in-between.

the book

She rises from the corpse and stumbles into the remains of a once solidly wooden pew. She sits, looking forward towards the unused and dusty altar, wondering at what god may be about and if this place is still holy to them, or if it ever was. The fallen's last breath still circles within her, leaving her momentarily groggy like any good drunk once they've reached their happy capacity and their mind is properly befuddled and fogged.

She intends to rise and leave this place. She begins to stand but finds she's a little unsteady of her feet for a brief moment causing her to stumble a bit. Her stumble dislodges the pew she'd grabbed on to for balance. It causes something to fall to the floor from the pew's back pocket where normally the prayer books full of psalms are placed for the faithful.

She mostly ignores it, or tries to, by tapping her fingers against the seat of the pew she has reseated herself. Her foot nervously hammering away at the end of her leg does her no good. In an "aw fuck it" moment her resistance crumbles and surrenders to her curiosity. The puzzles to a book that should not exist here is too irresistible to be left alone.

She peeks under the pew and sees a beat-to-hell book lying open on the floor. She drags it over to her using the toe of her boot to where she can pick it up thinking to replace it in the pew's back pocket. The book's spine is broken and it insistently falls open to pages 126 and 127. She closes it, before placing it back in its vacated space on the back of the pew, putting the world back to its rightful order once more.

She means to ignore the book which seems mostly whole as compared with all the other psalm books there The once fallen book now replaced stands out against the backdrop of the other crumbling and decaying books as she surrenders to the oddity of the book and pulls it out to take a closer look. She's mildly surprised to see that it's a copy of that old Stoker book smeared with mud and bloated from the waters which have recently receded and smelling like it too. The smell is decay, mildew and disturbed wet earth which she finds appropriate for this particular work. The pages are torn and frayed and its spine broken in more than one place. Investigating a thought, she drops it and finds that it falls once again to pages 126 and 127. She wonders how it got here in this old church. She briefly wondered if it had arrived with the cooling corpse, though this seems unlikely considering its placement high in the pew and how he only recently arrived.

She's still fighting back the insatiable curiosity, the one drawback to her current condition, or the only one she's currently aware of. The curiosity causes her to drop the book a few more times and it always lands back to pages 126 and 127. Curiosier and curiosier it draws her interest to what might be so important on this particular page versus its opposite. Taking a closer look at page 127, she sees a quote underlined in red with the addition of exclamation marks to add to the already implied emphasis of the original underline.

The quote on the troublesome page 127 is about the nature of death and the accompanying frightfulness of her approach. She herself knows a thing or two about this of late considering her most recent encounter with Death;

but it also tells of benevolence, which is something she feels she may have missed when she'd been passing through. Apparently even Death offers some relief from her scarier aspects, or at least on this insistent page. She finds it a strange quote to be so strongly emphasized and yet it resonates with her as she closes the book, placing it in the pocket of her coat without any why to her action, other than it felt like the right place for the book to be, like it had always been meant for that pocket.

She contemplates the irony of finding this book here in this formerly holy place, appreciating the oddity of it. This book which she'd never read before, having never really gotten into that Gothic vibe. Though this certainly seemed like a good time to start, like at page 127 and that persistent quote rattling around her brain. She pats her pocket satisfied with the mystery unraveled, before stepping to the end of the pew, over the unfortunate at her feet, down the aisle and out the doors into the cold, cold night.

due diligence

He of the ungodly hour phone call had been given the assignment that no one wanted. All agreed the assignment was a career sinker and was best for all if it would go away. These, of course, are exactly the kinds of things which will never go away by wishing of course. They're the type of things that take hard ugly work, done by men of the same character or at least characteristics to see through to the end of. He was neither of these things. He was, if anything, even more like all the others who'd not wanted this thing and so therefore, by simple inference, he wanted it to go away as well. Another freaky case that most wished had died as the still-born thing it had most obviously wanted to be.

He was rumpled and unshaven looking like a walking, breathing example of the phrase, 'like hell.' His appearance was appropriate considering the most recent past combined with the hour of receipt of the aforementioned unwanted phone call, bringing him here to this moment and to this unwanted assignment. It was his to pursue and whether he actually exercised due diligence was unnecessary and unexpected of him. His sole purpose in these events was to make it go away. Quietly and quickly being the preferred methods to all others. He finds himself wishing for a cigarette, a habit he'd long thought behind him and buried way back when.

all kinds of things

They call her evil, a killer. Even dare to utter psychopath, sociopath, and other pejorative descriptors, saying all kinds of things about her. All kinds of things are said, but never an actual name or identity. Adverbs galore, hyperbole occasionally, but no name for her and none asked for. She rather prefers it this way, having no name or identity to cling to her, nothing of note that might identify her in this or her previous life. 'All kinds of things,' said and each one interchangeable with the next phrase which might pass any lip. One thing was as good as another, as fitting as anything else, making it little to no matter which and what of whether kinds of things were said about her.

It's all so many words and words fill every day in print, TV and online, and none of them really mean anything. So feel free to utter anything at all, anything you dare from the column marked 'all kinds of things.' One word of advice for you, if you'll allow, if you can spare a moment from your parsing: please know it's the mark of a wise person to know when and where to deliver their words. The whole know your audience cliché. 'All kinds of things,' now being her own personal category and one never knows when she might take offense. So please, do feel free to exercise your rights to speech and press, but also perhaps, choose carefully when selecting your time and place to utter 'all kinds of things.'

Kiss

Heaven and Earth

Burn

Tonight her city burns. Three days ago it flooded. A dead would-be looter lies outside her door, though it is not her kill. She doesn't think it out of any real sense of, or of any kind of morality, or denial of the crime. It's more like, 'he was dead when I got here,' kind of thing. Even that's incorrect: had she been here she would have killed him, 'thou shall not take what's hers motherfucker.' This is the only kind of morality which matters in a situation like this.

But back to her first statement, her city burns. You may've seen it on CNN or whatever, gathered safely in a clutch, like hens in a nest. All of you nodding in agreement about the tragedy of it all, even as you turn around for one last grab at the donut tray. She can feel what you would call a wicked little grin as it crosses her face. 'Oh yeah,' she says right back into your face so you cannot mistake that she's talking to you. Talk to her when it's your city. She may not be from here originally, but she was found here, she was born here when she died here and here she'll stay.

Tonight her city burns. She watches the colors catch the sky and glow off the bellies of helicopters dotting and crisscrossing the sky and there's little she can do about it. She tries to swallow, wishes to empty lengthy curses at whatever gods will hear them, when they've already collectively allowed such a thing to happen to the people and the city. Strangely, ironically, this makes her glad, for now she knows her purpose and it's this city. Let this serve as a warning then. She will not tolerate. This is her manifesto, her threat and her promise, a warning and the only one at that, that's it. There's no interpretation or nuance to be found. There's nothing to negotiate and it's not open for discussion, she will not tolerate. So if you come to her city mark it in advance, note it somehow, someway. To those already here consider yourself served as they say in the parlance: *she will not tolerate.*

thin line

This is not where this story begins, though this is where it starts. It begins in the past, in a non-history which exists and is important now because she so happens to still be beating at the pavement under foot. That's another point of contention, a small bone to nit-pick to death. The dead have notoriously odd senses of humor. It wasn't her idea to come back, mind you: she'd been quite happy where she was. Now most of her actions are a making up for lost time kind of thing, a reverse redemption, in a twisted fashion of willfulness. A measure of answering the question asked: if one can die in a manner unbefitting or unequal to a life lived, then why not at least live a life to match the demise earned?

Admittedly, this is a point that's much clearer once you've crossed the very thin line which marks the boundary between this world and that one and not once but twice, and see how ridiculously, how easily it *is done*, not can be, but *is done* and then back where she's found herself now in the in-between. She's realized now, how ludicrous it was for her to not have experienced everything she could, and feeling a need to squeeze every last little piece of living out no matter the decadence or the level of criminality involved.

She didn't feel subject to rules anymore, to any questions of right or wrong. She didn't want to discuss or quibble over such subjective things anymore. There was only the in-between, her manifesto, and whatever else she could take and claim for herself.

rise

She wakes in an abyss without any light, not even a hint. There's no air which doesn't worry her as much as you might think, as she's not breathing. There's a deathly cold all about her, but she senses this is true more than she can actually feel the cold. There are no tell-tale signs of breath hanging in the air because again, she's not breathing. What she feels she doesn't know. There's an overwhelming sense that this is not right, that nothing about this is right. She seems to be conscious, seems to have some segments of evidence that would indicate life but this doesn't seem like living which leaves her the one real option. But it doesn't feel like death either. Not that she has any real prior experience mind you.

She feels claustrophobic and reaches out with her limbs to find herself entrapped in a long slippery steel square of a box. Now she really freaks out, fighting back panic as she tries to process a situation that she has absolutely no background for. There's nothing she can reach for above or behind her to help her in her present state. She reaches up towards she doesn't know where and starts to run towards a possibility, not because she knows what she's doing but because it's slightly less frightening than her present situation.

She slams her hands and arms upwards, kicking out below her with her legs. She thinks to scream but it catches in her throat when she remembers she's not breathing and so has no air to give voice to any scream and only the enclosed space to offer it to anyway. She again reaches to the bottom of her prison and kicks away from it with a strength she did not possess in life. Her arms are stretched out above of her with her hands cocked into fists. She explodes through what feels like a small door, slamming past it despite its protestations and lands roughly upon a hard and cold tile floor.

All is dark and silent except for her head and her heart, which are both screaming at her to get out, get out, get out! This is a fine sentiment except for one little tiny detail: she doesn't know where she's at. It seems very much like a morgue, but if this is true then why is she ambulatory? Another of the many annoying questions she doesn't have answers to but must push to the side for now to allow some kind of animal instinct to take over. She tells herself to save those kinds of rambles for a later time when she can process them. Right now there's only the need for escape and flight, followed by a search for safety.

She scrambles as she slips on the tile, fighting for traction but none comes under foot. She reaches up with an arm to pull herself to a standing position and force unsteady and possibly unready legs underneath her. Her hands push against a cold steel table as she forces her shoulders up and backwards as she fights like a skyscraper to reach her full height. She hears bone and sinew snap back into rightful places as tendon and muscle scream at the pain, realizing how she seems taller now than she remembered being. Her body is shaking as her brain fights off the assault. She doesn't know how much time has passed until she realizes she's standing and her hands have somehow imprinted themselves into the steel of the table.

She carefully relaxes her grip and breaks her hands free from their entanglement, staring like an idiot at them, trying to figure out if they're really part of her. Still in disbelief, she commands them to rise so she might look at them. Her knees buckle at unremembered lightness and she looks away from her hands to confirm two things. One: she is in fact standing. And two: this room is what she'd first thought it, a morgue. She catches her reflection in the steel of the table beneath her strange hands and sees pale, so pale, ghostly flesh reflecting back at her. She reaches out her hand to touch the reflection afraid she'll make it disappear like breaking the surface of the water. At the same time she's scared it will not ever go away. She understands somehow this is the real her now. She's not even bothered by her own nudity or the absence of vaguely remembered wounds, nor the tell-tale marks of healing on her body.

Her ears stretch their range out farther than they've ever reached before to question after something she thought she'd heard. She turns her new-found hearing to a quick scan of her surroundings for things she might use for her immediate purpose of escape. So pressing is the process of flight, she doesn't bother to stop or pause to question the 'how' of her processing these events. These very strange and seeming impossibilities in so calm and accepting manner. So many things going against her prior nature and yet a part of her new nature, a nature that flows effortlessly from her as though she were born to it and yet she knows she was not. At least the person she used to be was not.

The first priority other than escape itself is clothing. Not as a mark of modesty so much as a necessity. Even in this present state, her mind can process: she finds an overlarge pair of scrubs in some god-awful pale sea-foam-green. Though ugly as sin, the scrubs serve the purpose of fitting her without the worry of sizing. Clothing seems superfluous when she isn't feeling the temperature as she should were she alive. Nor does the ever present sense of self-consciousness or perhaps shame, she had before finding herself in this state.

Now dressed, she feels the need to dash, to run, to get through the doors of this place which is so much like a prison, or a coffin. She wants to be out of here and to get underneath the stars and the night sky. In her haste to get outside she once again doesn't pause to consider how she knows it is night outside. She tears for the doors and blessed freedom, hearing her bare feet striking a steady beat against ancient linoleum.

She hits the crash bar on the doors with such force that the door springs out and then back with enough force to smash any normal person who might have still been in its path. But she's not there. She's gone, already a block down the street and can still hear the crash of the door as it slams back into its frame. A giddy laugh gurgles up and bursts from her throat to echo though the city night with stars above her head. Her haunting laugh bounds throughout the corridors of the city as she sucks in the very first breaths of this new existence. She heads off in no particular direction, she's glad of the freedom and unsure of where or any idea or concept of home.

The night air tastes delicious as it offers up a different spice than she'd previously known. There is a bouquet of scents and sensations that prickle against all five of her senses and a few other senses that she has no words for besides 'new.' Over all of this is the sense of being so alive. More alive than she's ever felt before, without any understanding of the state she's in and a question she knows she'll need answers for. But those are clouds out on the far edges of the horizon and not meant to be dealt with now.

She feels a strength she's never known before. A new power in her arms and legs as it flows throughout her person and back to its source at the core of her being. Beneath her breastbone she can feel it radiate out from her in a circle all around her. Later, she'll see how it affects people near her; how crowds will literally part before her, as if she had criers ahead of her shouting at the top of their lungs, 'Make way! Make way!' But this is but one of her new powers and it only newly discovered and not understood. Other powers will come, though she'll never feel she has a complete understanding or a control of how they work. They will be there at her command all the same.

funeral

There was no crying at the funeral and it was poorly attended. It's difficult to have a funeral when the body has gone inexplicably missing from the morgue. It's not like a body can get up and walk away, but there is no other explanation offered or asked for in these chaotic days barely removed from the storm to explain the absence of a body. It's simply accepted with a shrug as people move on to more pressing matters. Still, if this scene were lifted from a movie, there surely would have been rain and some sad, mournful music to accompany it.

There were none of these things, but then, what can one expect when there is no guest of honor, no main attraction. A fake funeral cannot expect much more without the guest of honor. She knows she's mocking and that its rude behavior for the setting but then, it was to have been her funeral after all.

It's a singularly strange moment to witness your own burial and subsequent rites (such as they are), even if at a distance from the sparse audience. It would not do to be recognized, after all, as an attendee at your own last rites. It was a sight she strangely did not want, as some strange form of reverence had slipped through all of her glib and shallow, if typical, mockery. Closure is the word the psychologists would use, but it was confirmation which she was looking for. Some proof wanted by her, of how she'd indeed, moved on from this world and truly into this new existence. There were only a few lines for her in the local paper but key to these was the last line declaring "no survivors." Truer words seldom found. No survivors, but here she is in stark contrariness, in pure defiance to all of the known natural laws: here she stands.

"Christ" she thinks, "but the Irish have the right idea." The idea of an Irish wake sounds particularly good to her right now. If she's to slip into melancholy, she might as well lift a pint in her own honor. She looks to crawl into a pub to confess her most recent blaspheme to the bartender/high priest. If nothing else, it would put a pause upon her mockery.

Fire and Water

tears of heaven

It's not rained since the storms. Twenty-one days without rain which seems strange in this land where it rains almost every day. She supposes there's an irony there as well, for one to ask for rain, for more water after a flood. But the city needs the rain's cleansing power to help clear away some of the residual effects that line the streets. The gurgled up debris and detritus still marking the city, still laying its claim upon its captured treasure, reluctantly and infrequently surrendering it back. 'Tears of heaven' as some poets have called it. If you go for that kind of prose, if there is any other place on earth right now which is more befitting any tears, she doesn't know it.

Look at her now getting all mawkish. Such an easy thing to do as it's been said how the dead are notoriously sentimental. But do not expect a tear at the corner of her eye, let alone for one to fall upon her cheek, as she no longer remembers any reason why she should cry. It's a permanent disconnect remembered like a severed limb, all phantom and ghostlike, gone though you can still feel it. This is as maudlin as she's capable of getting anymore, past the wide swath of disconnect for normal things, living things. Damn, she thinks, she misses the rain. She's always loved a good hard rain despite the recent storms. Irony and sentiment are the true curses of the dead. They both become so suddenly clear that you cannot believe how you could have missed them at all in the first place.

whiskey

Feels like whiskey tonight. There are some aches and pains which only Jack can medicate. She gives up her watch for the date with Jack, no one can be forever vigilant. Sometimes needs must be met. There is only so much one can do after all. Besides, it was turning into a dreadfully slow and deadly dull night anyway. She's feeling mean, hence the whiskey, because it dulls the edges and produces better memories - or at least softer dreams. With enough Jack there won't be any dreams at all, which is best of all. This is, of course, a fingers-crossed kind of hope on her part here as her dreams were never satisfactory before and in recent times have taken a decidedly stranger turn. Such are the penalties one must serve when surviving so close an encounter with the other side.

Her forgotten scars suddenly seem to rise up to a visible state past any ability to ignore them. She blinks her eyes once, twice and her skin returns to its familiar porcelain state. The sight even if imagined is yet another good reason for whiskey. There's an old saying that hardly and yet uniquely does apply to her here: she wants to crawl into a hole and die beg your pardon. More irony she knows, but time enough for all of that later, she's got to go. Jack's calling to her after all.

drunk

Just remember, no one sets out to get that drunk. Possibly, for her it's a painkiller but there's never enough to actually kill the pain making it an ironic application. Another kind of lie, and though kind, Sir Jack chases and dulls all the pains, even the ones which are strictly remembrances and not actual pain, it's never permanent. Somehow the pain comes back harder, sharper and stronger than before, phantoms all sure, or so she tries to tell herself. A cruel trick or maybe more irony, she'll never know the difference. She stumbles forward and looks at the remnant near the bottom of the bottle with a mixture of hate and allegiance. She comes back to the conclusion of the night before and it all points to the same thing. It's the call to the hunt too long ignored, too long delayed but the moon and the stars demand it. Her blood calls her to it and demands satisfaction so tonight will be a hunting night.

fire

A person walks with a gas can in hand, not so unusual a sight around the city these days, with so many generators to create the artificial light. Except, there is no din of noise from any generator nor is there any generator to be had. This is a 'play with fire' situation. She's thinking pure 'live by, die by' in her head, if this one likes fire, she will let him set his fire and then she will let him die by his own work – fire the purifier.

Shit! Things are getting too biblical or mythological or something, around here of late and then maybe there both one and the same god-damned thing. Fire and water, water and fire, look at us; we've been reduced back to our most basic elements, stomped back to ancient fucking times. When you're stuck in the in-between, things become such a blinding blur; they fall out of any kind of rhythm. A disconnect from the real time or any real sense of it at any rate.

She wants a big fat cheeseburger: a real burger with a fat slice of tomato and a quarter inch slice of onion with both brown and yellow mustard and maybe BBQ sauce.

The kind of burger that you need two hands for and not that faux shit the corporations would fob off on us.

Got to focus else she'll make poor work of the fire starter. Dammit though, it's already too late and the kill's done. She should feel ashamed or something she thinks, perpetrating this action without realization and all the while thinking of a damn burger at that. If she were a pondering sort she might stop and wonder at the person, no check that, the very *thing* she's become - perhaps evolved to. She doesn't know and evolved seems too strong a word, too sophisticated a concept to describe the situation she's graduated to. Those are the types of questions to be saved for the Man of the Waters but he'll have to wait until after the burger.

Port of Call sits on the far edge of the Quarter away from where the tourists go which is all the better and serves the best burgers in the city. She sometimes wonders if in some crazed version of Roget's Thesaurus if tourist is not somehow a version of parasite? Sorry about the biting cynicism there. No pun intended she swears, but her PC gland did not return with her from the great beyond. Maybe it's the hunger talking or maybe she's still feeling a little bit mean from the other night. Nothing that a fat cheeseburger cannot cure and so off she goes.

man of the waters

The Man of the Waters and never a man better named. He is a big man with braids in both his hair and his beard. Think of the phrase 'still waters run deep' to get the idea of what his chosen form looks like. This man who seems ancient and young all at the same time, has been sentenced to serve as some sort of moral conscience for her, though he doesn't seem to begrudge her the servitude. It was he who offered up the first clear definitions on this new existence of hers. He is always good for a clarification, even if he's not always clear. She walks with the intention of going down to cast her troubles along the river in hopes of drawing his attention this evening.

She feels for the old bastard being stuck with her to talk to, but he is inherently and infinitely patient. Benefits perhaps of being theoretically ageless though she imagines for him it's not so much theory as fact and perhaps far beyond to plain "is." The Man of The Waters: eternal and forever rolling on, unheedful of the strike of clock past the once great city of New Orleans. The strike of clock being their common point of reference from which to begin when she wanders down to bring her midnight confessions to him, metaphorically speaking mind you. She heads on down to where the river touches the land, past the Governor Nichols Wharf into a dark corner of the river.

There's no telling if the Man of the Waters is in a talking mood. There's no telling if he's even listening and still she tells her latest woes to the dark brown of the river. She throws her words out over the water whether the Old Man is listening or not to let the river carry them away as it lays beneath the partly open skies without a moon or stars, undisturbed by electric light. There are no answers or responses to what has turned into her soliloquy, though she still walks away feeling better simply for the telling, granted a moments relief from the burden.

She won't call this confession, despite all the obvious allegorical and anecdotal evidence described previous. She doesn't believe in confession, never has. There seems little sense for it now, and hell, little reason to go round labeling it. She never was a deep thinker previously, but lately she's had nothing but time on her hands. She moves forward like the rest who wander here caught in the in-between. So call it what you want, she doesn't know other than she's done and gone.

Ash and Blood

murder

M-U-R-D-E-R-E-D. Murdered. The voice or
thought echoes from deep in the darkest spaces that lie at
the back of her mind, or from across the universe for all
that she knows, or more accurately doesn't. Too much of
that lately, too many holes and blank spots of simply not
knowing, not the past, not the now, certainly not any kind
of future beyond the next hour or so.

Perhaps this is what shakes her so much, having this
one clear thought screaming so suddenly loud and clear
with a conviction she cannot ever recall ever having
experienced. She doesn't know yet if it's a help or not to
know so strongly now that she's been murdered. Not

when everything else has so far been so elusive to her, refusing any clarification of this new existence of hers.

It seems suddenly contradictory to have received this explanation for how she got to this point, while also so thoughtfully providing an impetus which is so damned strong it could almost be called a purpose. It won't be, because it chafes to strongly at the concept. It goes against the chaos she's been so recently enjoying.

She's infuriated with the clarity of this one word as compared to everything else in her in-between existence. This brief flash of new information gives her a beginning for the narrative which she was already well in the middle of, and now she has to go back to the start and re-evaluate all she's been and done prior.

Luckily, she's neither a deep thinker nor a reflective person so she can skip that pile of bullshit and focus on what knowing she was murdered can do for her now. What it has done has given her a glimpse of the persons to whom she can make her wrath known. The perpetrators who have earned the mark of her vengeance which will start this very night. It's more fuel for her barely controlled anger, her rage at the act done upon her. It's not about noble truths like justice or law or any higher concept. It's about being pissed and having the means to do something about it, to alter the course if you will. She enjoys the thought as she grabs her blacks and her leathers about her, laughing as she steps out into the night and the hunt both waiting upon their mistress.

time

The world has taught her not to want or to ask or to wish for things. One must take what they want and must do so when and where one can. The world doesn't ask for forgiveness and neither will she. She understands how that comes off cold and yet, there it is all the same. She will lay claim to every last little piece of life she can. She will ignore all definitions put to her actions, deciding for herself on the matter of debauchery. She will be the sole arbiter in matters right or wrong, of all subjective. There will not be any quibble or discussion over such trivial things, such small concepts now that she's well over the thin line and past these concepts, deep into the in-between.

This is her response to the question previously asked: if one can die in a manner unbefitting or equal to the life as lived. Why not at least place a life lived before said death to at least show that you earned your demise. In death she will earn her demise. She will make up for it in spades or buckets or whatever other measure you choose or cliché you prefer and no time like the present as the saying goes.

She will fill up the in-between with everything she can to make up for what she'd missed in the period between her natural birth and death. They're nothing more than roads to and from those two points and everything else is the fill, the chase for pointless meaning in a time marked mostly with fear. Frightening the prospects of living, of pushing life out to its farthest limits for fear of what comes next. When next could be so much nothing shouldn't one push harder in the now to escape the fear which is greater than the dark. We humans can ultimately find an edge to the dark, we can pretend we fight back against it, or at least define it with our electric or neon bulbs, awash with the colored, if artificial light, or our most primordial invention and second largest fear behind the darkness, one of man's favorite toys – fire.

Time is a phenomenon, a phantom, a concept, a rather good idea more than a measurable thing. Especially when you live in certain places, places like the city of New Orleans. If you've never been there you cannot understand and if you have, and you were out well past midnight, then you know all too full well what's meant. There are places in the Quarter which only appear in the darkest parts of both location and time. They cannot be found by find looking or by the light of the sun.

Time is a luxury, an indulgence and certainly not a reliable measure. Its importance becomes lost as you sink into the deeper Quarter, into the deepest parts of her reaches. A slip past time and history in a city which is never still nor a part of the modern age. She's an entity unto herself, with her own rules and rights and rites with a disregard for timekeeping, which is a profession and measure without meaning in this eternal place.

It can make things confusing if you fight it. It can drive you mad if you seek to change it. Most importantly it makes it very easy to become lost, to lose all bearings and meanings if you cannot recognize the rhythms and signs the city provides, all along a route unmarked by the concerns of time. Becoming lost is not so hard here in this city; to lose all track of time is not so hard in this city; to be outside of space and time is not so hard in this city. New Orleans is perhaps the largest track in North America standing between worlds, caught in the in-between as she knows it, as she feels it and understands better now. A sisterhood, a kinship with one foot in the Father of the Waters, and the other in the slipstream of time.

pain

Her body hurts and aches every time she wakes with the memories and haunts of injuries past and present, and the promise of future wounds to come. They're not real mind you, just memories, or perhaps suppositions of what she has wrought. She rises to whatever hour it is, unconcerned with such trivia as night or day. The aches will disappear and the hurts will dull to a low throb, like a constant humming sometimes ignored.

A touch of Jack can soothe this humming down to no more than an inconvenience. A blurred reminder of what she has been.

Pain, it's been said, is nature's way of letting you know you're still alive, though in this current incarnation it is perhaps a little less apt. Still, it's an interesting point if not a truth. Perhaps we are, all of us, nothing more than the totals of our aches and pains, minus the years we've lived or the years we've left. It's some kind of odd mathematical equation which cannot actually be solved; which cannot be proved or disproved, providing a never ending argument. A formula drying on weathered paper. She doesn't begrudge the hurts and aches. They've earned their place after all and deserve to keep them. Besides, she might not remember who she is without them. Were they to go missing, would she become someone she did not know, different and a stranger to herself.

There's a calm which comes over her. A stillness of clarity and purpose removed of all emotion and replaced with a cool objectivity, a welcomed presence. It helps her to sort through the chaos, to put order to the things she wishes to achieve. It's a feeling at once strange and wonderful; an odd combination to achieve this level of comfort with oneself and the new ways of the world.

memory

She remembers everything. She doesn't want to but cannot escape it either. She remembers everything is also a lie. Sorry. Too much whiskey last night, she's feeling damned sorry for herself. Self-pity and cry me a river, and try not to drown.

It's only since these new events where this remembering everything has become a truth for her, a new reality. Blessing some might say. She would sneer at them and call them fools one and all. She'd ask them if they'd ever considered that perhaps there were some very valid reasons for forgetting. Some things are too trivial or completely unnecessary to recall, and yes, some are too unpleasant or painful. Forgetting is a biological defense mechanism designed to save ourselves from ourselves, lest the mind fucks with our inner psyche way too damn much. She's completely lost the capacity for it now, and is rather glad of it. Being able to recall had seemed too much like being stuck in unbroken circles far too unpleasantly reminiscent of spinning hamster wheels.

Air and Breathe

surreality

Nearly seven months past the storms now and enough time to get over almost anything. She looks at pictures of images her own eyes have witnessed. Yet, she can somehow still not make herself believe these things have occurred or how they're all too real. It's too large a pill to swallow, even if it should be surrounded by jam or jelly and refuses to go down easily. It's all too surreal to accept as reality or as happening to you. Sometimes she likes to amuse herself with the thought process which not even Dali himself could have imagined living day to day in this surrealistic paradise. Look around this should not be reality. This is what happens to other people in other places, but not here. No, not here, and not to us here, not in this place, and especially not to her.

Evidence is in plain view every damn day. You don't have to look far to find it. Hell, you don't even have to go out of your way, look or stroll down the block. Every one of us, everyone around has gone through the same experience and yet they have not. The storms with their very natural randomness victimized us all, but none of us equally. She cannot and doesn't dare to speak for others in their individual experiences.

All she asks for is a stop to the ranking of the hurts on this absurd scale, as if somehow, in some perversion, it makes a person's very individual pain lesser or greater than the next persons in a patently unfair fashion, but then so too were the storms in their passing and the distribution of their results. The fact she's still standing doesn't in any way affect the details of your circumstance. She's not to blame for living or for anything else despite the irony inherit there in the thought. She needs to step off of her soap box and the waxing philosophic. Such are the perils in this confusion she finds herself in. This strange land of in-between dressed before a Daliesque landscape.

Hell, maybe she needed a night off, a night to go out and get drunk or laid or both. Even a half dead like her can have desires or needs of a still earthly variety. A shocking thought of language or notion these thoughts and desires. They are not as far removed as you might wish or think and have nothing to do with dead or alive or only half dead such as her. There are no real distinctions in the series of blurred lines lining this side of the curtain. No clear delineations or definitions offered let alone a chance to explain. It's as simple a thing as she wants what she wants and tonight she has a terrible itch to scratch so time to go now.

the news

Killings make the news, though not as much as one might think they would or even should. Another vital if useless statistic ever dutifully reported, as if it's no more than a blip and now, the weather they state with their stone faces in an always awkward transition. It's so glossed over, hardly anyone notices. It causes almost no one to raise their head in any form of acknowledgment of the deed, let alone raise a voice against the violence involved in said deed. Protests are occasionally offered up, some strange form of futile protest. No one feels any earnestness or a real sense of pressing need to actually affect *real* change. Yes, killings make the news. They are ever so carefully reported to keep the population in check. Here, in this city it's a regularly sad duty dutifully recorded with the five, six, and ten o'clock news. Perhaps a lead item and perhaps not. It's only really news when there's not a killing to lead off your local news offered up five times a day and there's the truth behind the news if you could hear it.

The level of ambivalence does at least offer her one benefit. It allows her work to go largely unnoticed. It becomes lost in the natural phenomenon more commonly called noise. More noise in the chaff of the numbing regularity of any particular activity. This one happens to go by the name of murder. Even Shakespeare once noted the phenomenon in his famous phrase by which we call etcetera. There her blasphemy as such stops for the moment, though blasphemy may be too strong a word for it. It's not like she has any relations with any deity, and was mostly thinking about ol' Bill over the point. She realizes suddenly she meant plagiarism, so she had the wrong phrase there. If she were more demure, she would offer up a fancy bow of subservience to beg forgiveness, but those are no longer feelings she associates or acknowledges kinship to.

legends

Lies damned lies, half-truths and remarks uncorrected with the lie of omission which some would call the worst kind. They're deluding themselves there and she calls delusion the worst kind, but she digresses. Never before now has she ever witnessed the actual moment of creating the fiction. Her legend and reputation grow and if they continue unabated will soon rise to heretic proportion or out of proportion depending upon your viewpoint she guesses. Either way they might go, they will seemingly explode upon the limelight especially now in the information age.

Her reputation, if it continues on this pace will soon outgrow, if it has not already, from her own actual actions. Already things are being said and reported which she knows she's not done. She was not the one in the moment; the credit for it is unwarranted and undeserved. But then, maybe she's not alone in walking these paths. Perhaps she's not alone out on these streets and despite not having seen these other creatures should they exist, should they be. She walks her path alone despite all of the other creatures going bump in the night and about the city. These copycat actions are merely every damned strange occurrence being forwarded to her address as explanation. Acts of humans against other humans without any need of the mostly indifferent crowd walking along with her in the in-between.

It's a mostly moot point and she turns to a comforting adage at these little moments of doubt which strike with rare irregularity. The adage is what saves her each time and calls for her to not lament what she's wrought, what she's become by her own habits and hands. There's no returning to the beginning like some twisted film noir to undo with newly acquired insight or knowledge the actions which have caused her to be here in this place now. Things cannot be made or undone, assuming, of course, she would or should wish things unmade and she does not. She finds this situation suits her fine. It's just as well when there's no going back let alone the want to do so.

bad intentions

Time to turn to her blacks instead. To the nights embrace and a kiss of moon and star to light her hunter's path and to her prowl as she goes looking for trouble and is soon accommodated. A very large man with bad intentions makes her acquaintance after some not so careful prodding. Correction, provoking is, or would be, the more appropriate word to use for her portion of the action.

They're in one of those dark corners so conveniently accessed or commonly provided deep in all of the parts of New Orleans, but most especially here in her heart, the Quarter. He has her, he thinks, in a precarious position. Her back is to him and she faces an unyielding, unforgiving wall. His goal is unchanged as he starts to tear at the resistant denim of her jeans. She flirts briefly with the idea of letting him continue on his quest for savage love, it has rather been more than a little time for her. But then with a wicked little grin playing briefly across her face, she has a change of mind as sudden as the appearance of the idea of savageness.

He lunges after her again but she's not there. Instead he gets to eat some wall until a kick arrives at the back of his knee dropping him to his own. Another kick follows smashing into his kidneys with one last quick punch to the back of his neck. This last strike provides his face and teeth the opportunity to meet with the wall again. He then slides down the wall leaving a strange and sticky smear down along it to where he crumples into the street.

A small splash greets him as he meets the street to lie groaning in the muck which always lines the streets of the Quarter. She reaches beneath him and undoes his jeans. She pulls his pants and underwear down to his ankles laughing at her handiwork in an evil if ironic way. Not the way he'd imagined it she intoned.

She still feels justified in leaving him like this considering it was after all what he'd planned for her, tables turned and what not. She throws his wallet back down at him after she's retrieved what little cash he had before she strolls back out into the greedy streets and the cooling night's breeze coming up to caress her from up off of the river.

The Chase at Shadow

unwanted

The strikes come with near perfect randomness. He thinks of them as strikes, as assaults in a concentrated pattern if he can discover this pattern. The shear randomness of the events is what he finds unnerving. The calculated character to the randomness seemingly without rhyme or reason, made to look oh so perfectly like chance. Too perfectly executed he felt to actually be the haphazard activity it seeks to disguise.

He has to think there is a pattern which can be discerned, a process which can be discovered, or a mistake which she's made. Any grasp at straws which will lead him even an inch closer to his perpetrator. He has to think these things because no one else in the department will.

No one else even wants to consider it. He has to think these things, to give these events cause to ring within his consciousness; or else he too will fall to thinking like everyone else, and the case which would save him will become the case to bury him.

The case he did not want. That no one wanted. The strange-ass shit that was going down, that was too damn strange to not be unrelated but could not be related no matter how much thought and work he put into it. The case which all agreed, if silently, had to go away and no one wanted to touch because it was a career killer if ever there was one which was how he'd gotten it. The downward spiraling path taken by this strange ass shit to land on his desk. It could not kill his career because you cannot kill what's already dead. The walking dead is what his career had devolved into. He'd killed it years ago with the same clichéd sad story of drinking, bad marriage, a worse divorce, a little corruption (an institutional problem, don't let them kid you about it). These are not excuses or apologies. Hell they may not even be truths and there they are all the same, no escaping them. No escape at all.

This damned woman had to come in and ruin all of it. Here he'd been on the safe track to retirement, sure a disgrace to the department, but still with his badge. Still collecting his paycheck and before this, no one expected too damn much from him anymore. In fact, the less the better. And now the shit had finally shuffled its way down to the very bottom of the deck. She was his and his alone. If he could prove there was a she, an anything at all behind all these strange ass things going on in the city. A city noted if not downright famous for the strangest of all damn things.

He crushes two aspirin tablets between a spoon and the table. He then mixes them into his combination of whiskey and coffee in an uneven fifty-fifty mix that will not be divulged. The spoon swirls a mini-whirlpool into the concoction which, for the briefest of moments, seems to reveal his imminent future. Dark and cloudy and probably going to get him killed. He snorts back a laugh at the thought. Get him killed, it seems a joke, an improbability, the odds are not so much stacked against him as this coffee elixir currently is. Besides, gotta die of something and you might as well know what it will be.

Better that than this damn mystery woman, this spirit of vengeance in a city with every right to be pissed off. The woman with her singular knack of causing kills in a clear matter of 'reap what you sow.' It brings him to thoughts of Marie Laveau, the Voodoo Queen and protectress of the Crescent City. Lessons taught him when he was young and forgotten when he'd grown older, much to his detriment apparently. Could it be her or could it be her work or is it too much damn whiskey and not enough god damn sleep. Sleep the illusion, the fictitious dream if you will. The fabled land at this point in time and the quest which most in this city are probably after in the here and now called today.

Damn, but his eyes are burned out from this whole damned inconvenience, from too much which he has seen recently. Too damned much which cannot be unseen and nothing which Visine can wash away either. The heels of his hands rise to rub at his eyes as if they themselves could offer clarification which has otherwise gone missing. He's startled to discover a half burned through cigarette clamped between fingers stained from years of use. A habit thought behind him. A habit he doesn't remember picking back up let alone where and why. He stamps out the offensive smoldering thing and tries to tell himself he doesn't see the tell-tale signs in the smoke rising from the crushed offense.

If he thought he would believe it, he would tell himself he's not slipping. He would say to himself how his mind is still all there and intact, that sanity has not finally slipped from his grasp, lost in all of the madness around him. He'd continue to state how these things with the damned woman were true and could be solved. They can be found out. He chuckles again as he grabs up the concoction generously called coffee taking a large portion between his teeth. He'd promised himself he wasn't going to lie or bullshit himself anymore. In keeping with that promise from a million years ago, he cannot tell himself that anything he just thought was truth.

A sigh more like a ragged cough or an exasperation crosses over his lips. Another sign of death coming, she's not as scary as she used to be. He sets the coffee down. He picks up the bottle and shuffles away from the kitchen table with a screech of protest from a steel chair against the wood floor. He knocks the light to rocking and casting odd shadows as he wanders off towards the front of the house and the porch. He falls into a big overstuffed chair he doesn't remember owning though it's inviting and he gives in to it. The bottle finds his lips. The whiskey is sweet in color and taste with seductive promises of forgetfulness, offering a transport away from the pain and the memory, a ticket to sleep however short. Another swig and the bottle whispers a promise to take him away from it all. It's a promise he continues to search for til the bottom of the night.

Next morning, at least by his clock, finds him though he almost wishes it hadn't. Another wasted day to chase at ghosts, at phantoms, at demons. He doesn't want to know the news. Doesn't want to know what has occurred. Doesn't care whether she was out and about, or if she took the night off to let some other strange ass shit come to pass in the curved city of water and haunts old and new. He doesn't want to move, finds a curse upon his lips skipped straight past his mind. The curse is against the forces conspiring to keep him here in this life.

He raises his hands to wipe sleep away from his eyes an attempt to rub some life into him. He's shocked by how they appear, gnarled and some digits with fresh cuts red and angry some old and scarred many, many times over. He stares at them like they're strangers to him. They don't seem to be his hands at all. Today at least they don't shake. Today they're perfectly still and feel agile and powerful for the first time in as long as he can remember adding to the alienation from his own flesh. For a moment he forgets how old he actually is. Cannot remember the number though it seems it should be right there, readily available? Why would he forget his age or his hands?

He wants to stand. Wants to make his way to the bathroom, to a mirror to check, to reassure himself, this is still reality and he still dwells in it too. His hand rubs against the stubble on his chin. He stops his other hand short of pulling the switch on a light which might reveal something he doesn't want to see, acknowledge or know. Sight for sore eyes or perhaps the reverse would serve better. Not knowing because some things are better left unknown. He shuffles off to the bed for some more down time. He decides after checking his watch which never comes off, and sees it's still early and he can always catch her after dark.

shadows

She stretches forth at the crack of dusk. Her long limbs tumbling out in all directions as she stumbles up from the mattress lying upon the floor in the more or less center of the room which has remembered better people if not outright better times. Tonight presents some clarity for her. Tonight is the night in which pain reigns as only a memory promising to dim ever further with time. This comfort threatens to spiral into a manic moment, which threatens further mayhem. It's a strange and surreal if sudden companion to her place here in the in-between. If she were a more reflective type she would give pause. Instead she surrenders to the desire for mayhem. She rushes to embrace it as the door slams to her already gone.

He wanders the city with no set purpose or plans, only carrying with him his odd sense of duty. What to he couldn't tell you, though maybe it's to himself or maybe it's to the city he's always called home even during his tour in 'Nam. One last potentially more truthful thought passes through his mind. It's an unjoyful one about how this is for her like some strange vigil or service to her; an obligation faithfully observed. If she feels the need to haunt the city as its violent protector than perhaps he owes it to her, to the city, or himself to ride the dark hours with her and all of the other scares out prowling.

He sees her everywhere he looks. In every nook, every corner, and every twisted shadow which reside in the Quarter. He sips at his bagged tall boy trying to remain unclouded in thought, if not deed, as he wanders down towards the lower Quarter down river where the waters are dark and impenetrable. He passes Frenchman. A short walk farther down he passes a church where a man fell through locked doors and a little farther on into the apse the other day or was it months ago? Time never has had a strong grip on the Crescent City and it spells equally upon her citizenry and their memories.

Shadows flit and waver, being ever so careful where they must cross the light. All shadows except for one solitary, if determined, one which catches at the very farthest corners of his vision. He has a sudden flash of insight, a sudden quick inspiration. Perhaps it's a plain form of dumb luck or pure chance how he's the recipient of with the sighting of this stubborn shadow. He knows the shadow is her, or how the shadow can lead him to her though he is unsure as to the how of it. He'll never be able, in the future, to find any description for this moment when he tries to sort it out into any kind of a cognizant coherence. Those attributes were not to be found in this moment. They were not made for this event or for what followed.

He finds himself following the stubborn shadow without giving it another thought. This is the insight he's received. Follow and accept that which unfolds before you for it's a truth of the purest sort. He doesn't at first accept he trusts this feeling. But he has little choice in the matter. Has even fewer options available for him and this creature he's found himself inextricably linked to in some odd form of the tango. He decides to trust the insight. Trusts and even with his eyes closed he can follow the shadow. He can feel it pull and tease him along a path without end. He trusts and with each step the shadow becomes more. It becomes heavier and darker. It begins to have a tread and breadth, a scope and size.

He doesn't know, isn't aware of how long this dance goes for. He does find a familiar rhythm to it though. A beat known like it was his possessed or beloved. An item so personally marked as to never be lost though sometimes misplaced or forgotten, his. His alone or once was.

It's hers he realizes. Her beat he realizes he's somehow stumbled upon. This is his reward for the place of trust, the leap off into accepting the insight despite his skepticism at his own plan. He opens his eyes and can see with a clarity once reserved for his younger days. His thoughts are sharp and focused. His step assured for once in a number of years. It's this step which will take him to her; but only if he can remember to not question it for one moment more and take this one step.

gunfighter

Her laugh slips through the night. It slithers up into parts of his brain from which they'll never depart like a damned haunted mournful tune he swears he's heard once before. A tune which even now sounds like it's coming from a long way off. Like it's traveling a long way to be here for him now. It grows like a roll of thunder until it becomes almost as loud. Surprisingly it's not distractive, it heightens his focus, and it marks a new found element of resolve, with a determination now to go forth. One street corner more and with a little luck he will be rewarded, he knows it. He can feel it like the oncoming of rain which always triggers the old wounds from 'Nam in his knees and legs.

Down the street in a doorway she stands pressing something up against the wall. Delight and glee mark her features. Hell, she even seems to glow or perhaps it's some trick of the light. She's backlit and beautiful. She seems either unaware or perhaps blissfully uncaring if any should observe her here in all of her glory or gore, which are inseparable at a closer view. Suddenly he finds himself moving closer to her without drawing his gun or a thought given to the use of his police powers. It's a state indescribable in the moment but later falling somewhere between awe and pure curiosity or fascination, like watching a shark hunt or a bear strike.

She sees the man turn the corner to enter the street. She somehow recognizes him or his intent, even if he's lost it for a moment. She got lost in the hunt and had allowed this man's approach, and she'll later chastise herself about it. That's not for these moments here though, here and now action calls and action will hold sway. She lets her work crumple to the street before turning to face the intrusion. She moves into the provocative stance which recalls the gunfighters of old movies. This thought gives her joy written in a crease across her face in an evidentiary smile. A smile she's unaware is currently enjoying its own moments of notoriety and fame.

Her turn stops him straight cold in place. He sees her damn wicked smile cross her lips and swears her tongue follows across shortly afterwards. She stands starkly in the middle of the street in the classic invite to a gunfight pose. She stands unmoving and waiting for him he realizes, to do something, anything. He pushes himself up from a crouch he was unaware he'd been in and away from the building he'd been unconsciously leaning against. He steps to the street centering to face her in blatant disregard of fear and sense in equal doses. He somehow knows neither would be of help here anyway. Her smile grows at this and he's somehow pleased he's found acceptance from this monster, at his ability to gain her approval before shaking it away from him in disgust.

The night settles and calms in sudden apathy about the two who stand beneath her skies suddenly locked together in a détente and a link together neither would care to claim or know. They're unaware of the bond formed there by the laughing gods who find so much sport in all things occurring beneath their neglectful gaze.

He senses more than sees her move. Swears he feels her hand upon his cheek. A scratch of nails and she's upon him and filling all of his senses and then she's gone, gone like a whisp of never had been there. The absence is as equally crushing as her presence was a lifetime, a moment, a second ago.

Jack Kelly

Year and a Day

mourner

A year and a day is the traditional allotted period set aside for mourning. One year and one day. The agreed upon length of time deemed acceptable to grieve. Though when the date arrives, she finds herself unable to completely push her emotions aside however dull and foreign they may seem to her now. They're caught up in a larger more general turmoil which all but boils inside her. It churns as an untapped and unregulated rage threatening volcanic release if she's not careful about its application. That and the occasional careful bleed off which never lasts her for long when she turns all about her and her city, and sees so much that is still left undone and unfixed.

But she's searched and has found a right proper substitute for emotions a year and a day past due'. A right proper medicine in any dose through the embracing of her edict, her mantra, of non-toleration. She has fuel to burn as she strikes like a match hot in an instant flame from nowhere. Her first strike of flame occurs in the east, which is proper for a rising tide of red and orange to appear. She knows she must redouble and enlarge her efforts as they seem to keep skipping beneath the notice of the higher powers.

Things now like the darkness are closing in on her. Her little rebellious acts like a curtain are nearing the end of act four in a dramatic play. She can sense the end of things, but like any good script, she doesn't know how it will all play out. She sits at the edge of her seat like any other patron, biting her nails or would if she'd the habit. She wonders at the outcome until she's struck by so strange a thought it almost seems ridiculous. Another coat of surreal to paint upon this dream of hers. She can affect the outcome of this play if she tries hard enough and this is where memory kicks in and she recalls she's not only a player in this drama. She's the main player.

She's the protagonist in a work by her own hand. It leaves it to her as the agent who must affect the outcome. She's the principle on the set as it unfolds at her seemingly silent and unconscious command.

darkest part

All kinds of things, any names or labels you care to apply suit her fine. Who is she to quibble over any such characterizations. So many adverbs thrown at the dark unknown to see what sticks, in order to make familiar that bump in the night and perhaps scale down its ability to frighten. But what can she be then if she should choose to eschew labialization? If you must, if you prefer a definition, then try this: she's the haunt in the middle of the day that still calls to you in the night. She's that nasty lingering feeling that never, ever goes away.

Here's a thought for those of you of a philosophical bent, an exercise for you if you're of a mind. Perhaps she is what is found in the darkest part of night, but if she is, and you should then see her in the daylight, what then becomes for the two people thus caught up in implausible impossibilities? Call her evil if you like, but don't be surprised to find her standing on Holy Ground and in your shadow, taking the measure of your light. That cold tingle in your spine, that footstep from behind you without a person to claim it. The breathe on your neck or the low whisper in your ear, the scrape of a fingernail on your cheek. All these are her, are her mark if you truly wish to put names to things, to label, to call, to identify. It makes no never mind to her. 'Anything at all,' or and 'all kinds of things,' blending all together into remembrance or forgetfulness. It doesn't matter at all in the scheme of things and your continued need to call her will not stop her prowl in the night as she reinforces her law, in her city. She will not tolerate and she will be watching for you. You can count on that no matter which words you've chosen for it.

The Long Shadow

the chase after

He's getting closer to her. He finds it both alarming and satisfying in equal doses. He cannot prevent her from what she does. Hell, he's pretty sure he doesn't actually want that anyway. He does however think he's discovered that elusive pattern that his red-stained eyes have told him was there countless times before. If he could open his damned eyes and truly see, for once. He'd thought these things because he'd caught a glimpse of her in the night and now he knows, knows she's real. Then there was that damn strange business of hers down in The Marigny with the stranger collapsed upon a church floor. A church floor that shouldn't have been open to receive anybody, in a church that never saw attendance any more, even from before the storm.

He thinks he knows where she keeps her lair. He thinks soon he'll be able to put himself within reach of her. A grasp away followed by a shot in the dark and then this will all be over. He has no real way of knowing these things. He feels as if he has no right to them, an unearned sense of the turn of events misreading them as turned in his favor. It was more out of hope than any other thing except for his increasing sense of her as evidenced by their chance encounter from the other day now.

He wanders the streets at her favorite time of night. He too follows no pattern imitating her own behaviors, though he's begun to confine his jaunts to the lower Quarter and just off of it. Slightly downriver towards Frenchmen and The Marigny in mimicry of her own actions. This is where he's felt closer to her, closer to her thoughts, her steps, perhaps even her breath. He can feel her down here and there in the shadows. A street away as a blur barely made out. Signs she's near or has already passed, marked by people who look spooked or shook outright with a description which almost always matches down to the last detail especially if they, the unfortunate ones, had seen her eyes.

He needs rest, he needs a pause, and mostly he needs more coffee. He needs another chance to get this right but mostly he needs to know he's not crazy on this notion. He needs it to be over for himself and everyone else involved. No, scratch that and damn everyone else. It's a singularity now. It's all about her and him now. He's no longer even certain what he'll do when if he should find her. He has his doubts about the circumstances that have drawn the two of them within each other's orbits. Kill her? Sure, that's what's been wanted from the very beginning. It's what's best for all involved. That was the hard sell presented to him over the stinking pile of pure shit of this radioactive case was when it floated down to the bottom of the pile more commonly known as his desk.

He steps off the pavement into a darkened corner of a bar. The bar is sparsely populated by nothing more than the wannabes. The wannabe vampires and undead, skulkers lost in a city that welcomes the lost from anywhere and everywhere. No judgments passed as long as you keep passing on along.

He steps up to the stool empty at the corner of the bar waiting for the tattooed woman behind the bar to notice him. When she does, he gets a tall whiskey neat to keep him company. The first sip soothes with its comforting burn and he smacks his lips with satisfaction. A second lift of the glass soon follows containing a glimmer in the auburn liquid. A pale shake of light that should not be there flickers in the glass. It's still there when he raises the glass up higher. He sees a pale face shimmering up to the surface for the briefest of moments. So brief that no one will ever believe he actually saw it. He drops the glass as he turns spinning but she's not there. No one is there. He squints his eyes down tight and reopens them and still nothing. He picks the half spilled glass from the bar and there a blur comes again right up to the top of the liquid. "SHIT!" he says as he drops the glass again spilling more of the precious liquid against the bar. Enough of it splashes on his clothes to never convince anyone he had not been drinking.

He steps out into the street and starts walking letting his feet make the decision for him on which way to go. His head is tilted down as he concentrates on his feet for a moment. He's trying to alternately clear his head but also to make sense of the event witnessed. A laugh is carried along on the breeze from off of the river, except that there's no breeze tonight. The laugh is echoed up off of the street to knock against the buildings and into his head. He cannot get the damn laugh out of his head. He walks with the intention of heading home and getting some sleep but cannot seem to make it out of the Quarter. He looks about him and finds he's in a part of the Quarter he doesn't recognize. A part that he doesn't seem to know, which is an impossibility when he's lived here all of his life, but then maybe this is not his after all.

He steps into another bar to reorient himself. After a moment he swears he can feel her pass right next to him. He takes to the streets again and can feel her brush right up against him though when he turns she's never there. He makes his way to Jackson Square where he stops on a bench and lets the exhaustion overtake him. He allows it to hang on him in its attempt to drive him into the ground. He doesn't know, or later recall how long he was there on that bench with the night stubbornly clinging to him and the city. He will not be able to tell later how many people may have passed him as he sat there. Hell, he may not even be able to tell you *if* there were even people there.

Days and years pass in the minutes and seconds he sits there. He can feel the ages creeping up on him, threatening to overtake and claim their ultimate, if inevitable victory. He can feel the fight leaving him, the will to carry on in certain and abject defeat against an impossibility which seemed to grow more so. His breath becomes more ragged in its struggles to move through his body and out. His heartbeat slows to something which can no longer qualify as a rhythm, even if each beat pounds in his ears and head as a thudding alarm, louder and louder if slower and slower.

"Mon capitaine," a breath whispers into his ear as a startle, a tease. He doesn't initially move or give any indication that he's heard her, except for the tension that turns toward rigidness, the ever so slight tightening throughout his being, the only clue to point toward an auditory acknowledgment.

She seems to know otherwise. She seems to hear his every breath, every thought and heartbeat as she's within his very essence. It should be disturbing but it's not. Instead it's… it's alarmingly *arousing* and oddly there's some cold comfort for him there. It will be less to explain between them then. There's an inherent understanding of the situation and the roles they're playing here. Within this understanding is the silent agreement allowing them to play out the parts they've been assigned in mutual support of the charade.

"Cherie," she pronounces with the proper inflection. She presses her hand on his shoulder as a proof against the threat of anymore illusions between them. It acted also as a removal of any question of having his attention or not. He's still determined to resist her though, if only for one moment more. Wanting one moment more of resistance from her, one last second left in the fight for his own independence, his own freedom, his own pride more likely or the fear that if he turns to her too quickly he might himself be lost forever.

"Do you think to make yourself a hero?" Her follow up whisper in his opposite ear.

His head rises and turns to look over his shoulder to catch a glimpse of her. Her arm lingers with its

incessant pressure on his shoulder and chest as she
remains ever elusive to sight. This seems a clue, her
unwillingness to be seen. But then even he's not entirely
certain seeing her is of any positive benefit to anyone or
anything let alone him, lost on a park bench in the heart,
the very center, the ancient core of the city. He snorts
back a stifled gasp as he remembers that at one time the
ground beneath his feet was stained with the blood of
those who'd made grievous offense. This thought makes
the place of their meeting seemingly the more
appropriate. It's an old story about blood calling to blood.

"You have to stop," his voice gravels past cracked
and suddenly very dry lips. He can hear clearly past her
silence and a tack he thought wrong to take from the start
veers immediately off course. He's not struck his target,
has not found himself ground on which to negotiate or
fight. He needs to find the middle, a good enough as any
place to start from when attempting to come to a meeting
of the minds. His mistake here is thinking there's room
for negotiation, for mediation, a place for reasonable
people to meet. She will not accede any of these areas

though and he doesn't yet know that none of these are in play.

"They'll not let you continue on in this course," he tells her plainly but this too is greeted with more silence from her.

"You mean that you'll not," she states in a flat, if accusatory statement.

"Your escapades have escaped the point of being ignored or passed off as random things and there has come a demand for action," his reply.

"Do you think they'll appreciate you for this effort. That somehow by doing this you can find yourself a way back into their good graces? That you want that?"

"This is not about any kind of redemption," he replies.

"Oh, of course not," she says allowing for a playful pause out of mirth or contemplation he cannot tell the difference. "My apologies then, the general good is it then?"

something more

He looks to her still struggling to make up his mind about her. He's struggling with the nature of their mutual situation, at least shared from his perspective. He struggles to understand her, to find and know what question he might want to ask her now that they're here, face to face as it were. She creepily leans in over his shoulder her head cocked at an angle like she can read his thoughts. She seems to be trying to decipher his dilemma and comes away disappointed. She'd hoped for so much more from him when he'd spent all this time dogging her. She would sigh if she had but the breath for it.

His question the same as what so many others have wanted from her. The only question or query that ever escapes lips to ask her and it's always the same one of why. But there is no why and it's disappointing to her, a disappointment he can feel like a weight.

"I will not tolerate detective," she answers him preemptively. She knows this answer will not be satisfactory for its very nature. It's an answer so out of bounds versus what's normally accepted as allowable within a society. She can physically see him reject the statement before it can fully form from her lips.

"You're a killer," he finally says and this is so heartbreakingly disappointing to hear, she'd so hoped for something more from him.

"True," she says matter of factly, like the point is not even worth arguing, that it's beneath her really. She doesn't, has not, and will not deny what she has become.

"What gives you the right to do and decide these things?" He asks her and this is better than his first and completely unsatisfying statement. The words aren't his, they are the words of those who seek to have him do their bidding, but still it's a better try, "What makes you so different?"

"I grant myself the right detective," she almost spits out the declaration it being so easily answered. It's such an obvious response she almost deigns not to answer it because it was so far beneath her and beyond any need to explain herself. The second half of the question is not so obvious and there is a long answer to the matter but there's not the time to offer it so she goes for the short response instead.

"Who said I was so different," another answer that falls unbalanced into the discomfort side of the scales in all that it offers. He is visibly shaking now as he sits on the bench seemingly all alone as an arm untangles from his person. There is one last warm breath passing by his ear with whispered promises or threats. He thinks he might never know for sure about.

There's a long cast of shadow over and from behind him. It stretches across the pavement, across the stones of the square and reaches towards the door of St. Louis Cathedral. He swears for a moment as he sees the door open and the slip of shade stepping through inside before he comes to his senses. He realizes what an impossibility it would be with the Cathedral safely locked up for the night.

the mistake made

He'll wake the next day in his shorts and a battered white t-shirt lying beneath a fan sprawled upon his bed. The TV is still on in the next room of his shotgun. The house miraculously still standing after the storm and what came afterwards. He won't remember how he got there.

The empty bottle on the floor will cause him to question whether he imagined or hallucinated last night's encounter with that damnable woman.

It's when he stares into the mirror attempting to shave for the first time in an immeasurable period without a starting point that he can recall. He raises his chin and head to the left and sees an angry red mark on his neck where his neck joins his shoulder on the left side of his body. It's the same side of his body she'd leaned upon as she spoke to him in circular riddles. She's left an angry mark upon his skin and his first instinct is to be very pissed about it. He almost embraces this, and is well on his way towards full outrage, full on anger when he's seized by a thought. It's a thought so provoking as to be disturbing. It causes his body to shake for the second time in less than so many hours but this time he doesn't fight the shaking. He instead allows a raw laugh flow unforced past his battered lips to clear his conscience, his body, his mind, his soul.

She's straight fucked up, has made a mistake that he thinks to capitalize upon he tells himself. He hopes to spin it to make her a victim of her own cockiness. Hubris has taken hold of her and now will come back round to bite her in the ass. An ass he now owns. His laugh so ragged a minute ago comes out clearer now even as it provokes a coughing fit that shakes him to his core causing him to spill the cup of whiskey he doesn't remember pouring. Normally this waste would be a capital offense, but this morning he knows it will be the last he ever thinks of the ambered liquor. No more will ever pass his lips. He'll need a clear head in the days ahead as he steers a straight course to her. Oh yes, she's fucked up royally leaving her mark upon his neck for who knows what reasons. He would turn this mark of hers, this possessive statement of hers and reverse it. He will use this mark against her as it surely must.

You cannot leave a piece of yourself behind to only work one way. This seems like something she should've known. It's the one thought which gives him pause. Otherwise he's too excited about the possibility of error on her part for him to dwell upon the troublesome thought for long. He has a piece of her now, a piece of her she cannot shake loose. She thought to mark him and gave him something in reverse the other night. Her mistake in the mark she left upon him is what he hopes will give him a direct line back to her. This mark will be her undoing. Now he'll be able to really know what she's about or at least where she'll be and he'll finally be in a position to put her down. There are no more questions about it anymore, about undertaking that particular course of action. He doesn't even care anymore about the why or what or the other thousand theories about her. This has moved long past that point. It's a decision already made. The next time she stalks he'll be ready and he'll be the one to put the hunter down.

Man with a Gun

windmills

The hunt begins in the period of darkness before midnight. He allows himself to be pulled along down past the Quarter to some of the old warehouses that lay snug against the river between the Governor Nicholls and Poland Street wharfs much farther downriver. It's a stone's throw or more from any area where a tourist might dare to go with the sounds off Frenchmen drifting lazily through the night air. Off near a stretch where the hurricane did some of her worst. It is prime hunting ground for her. The moon is slung low in the sky to cast shadows, her allies in her ramblings.

She slinks through the shades of night. Her step feeling slightly misplaced, no, mistaken even as they carry her deeper into the heart of her city. Something seems out of place. Something's amiss though she cannot place her finger upon it. She feels infected somehow with something she cannot shake, like a fog lying low within her brain that muddies the waters to muddle the purity of her normally reliable clarity of purpose. She thinks to make it no matter, to shove it to the very back of her brain, to be ignored. It refuses to comply with these efforts becoming an incessant nudge that will not go quietly into the dark, seeking instead to tug at her, to distract her and weigh her down.

He hunches his shoulders up against some uncharacteristic cold and rubs his suddenly numb hands together to build some heat or feeling back into them. He has wandered for a short time now, but it's been long enough for the seeds of doubt to have crept up into the back of his mind as to his theory. He's not felt any pull from her. Has not sensed her having passed or been near any of the spots he's crisscrossed in the last hour or so and his doubt is now growing.

She comes across his path by accident as seems befitting to their little dance. When she sees him, she knows in an instant the reason for her discomfort in this otherwise fine evening for a hunt. She knows in an instant more where the pull all evening has been heading, bringing them both right here to put them both at this point, this cross of axis. Her head turns as if to cock an ear to a sound or voice which can just barely be made out at the edge of hearing. She cannot help but wonder if it's the gods laughing at her. She takes a quick step into a friendly shadow to ascend up the side of a squat if friendly small warehouse to a roof view of the river and lower Quarter.

From the corner of a down turned eye previously staring at his toes striking the pavement he sees a flit of shadow so small as to be inconsequential. He almost convinces himself he doesn't see it at all when an immense feeling of certainty floods his consciousness. He accepts this certainty without knowing why or caring to. He simply accepts this is her and knows it's a time now to make decisions however erroneous and not for any more questioning. Time to make a leap, a chase at shadows and now it's his turn for a flash of wicked grin as he turns to the chase, a tilting at windmills.

rooftops

Up a ladder scaled to a flat tarred rooftop where he finds his shade standing on the edge of forever. She seems to have always been standing there right where he expected her without understanding how he had been expecting it. Still the moment seems right between them up here on the edges between this and that, Caught on the eternal crossroads marking this precipice of the in-between. If he didn't know better he'd swear she'd been standing there waiting for him from time immemorial.

She doesn't look back at him. She doesn't make any move to hint or acknowledge his presence. She gives away absolutely nothing as her eyes and thoughts instead turn to the infinite clear sky. In a different frame of picture it would seem she was in a state of reflection or prayer but neither title suits here. It's simply the waiting, the pause, the short intake of breath before a needed if horrible course of inevitable events overtakes them both. She knows with a certainty the options before them here at this pivotal confrontation. She knows too with a sudden firm heavy grasp of pure exhaustion, a weight of fatigue, the only possible consequence that can be arrived at here. In a different light, she would seem saddened at the conclusion reached, but not this light, not tonight.

He picks the darker shadow out and separates it from the rest against the black of the night and roof. He reaches into his shoulder holster for the reassuring feel of the grips of his pistol. His gun is pulled and he's not entirely certain about the how or when of that decision; or about anything at all that should come next. Still he has the gun pointed at her before any real decision is made or considered. 'Dead to rights,' a phrase never more appropriately used or named, punctuating the point that it's his call. Assuming a voice can be found to make it.

Silence stretches farther than most people can grasp or believe. It can reach to parts and dimensions larger than thought and still compress with an immense pressure threatening to rend the very fabric of the world. Not even breathe can escape as sound disappears and the Quarter seems unnaturally still as one heart beat slows, and another starts to racing.

heroes

"Turn around," she hears and she can feel the gun ominously pointed if anonymously at her back. Her now trademarked wicked grin crosses her face as she wonders whether the gun is aimed high or low.

"Is that you Mon capitaine?" She says still smiling as she turns round. Her smile does little to assuage any fears he may have had. It worked instead to throw a cast of doubt onto his already dubious grasp of confidence. The confidential boost he'd received from the mark she'd left upon him, but then that mark had been intended as something potentially possessive and was thus probably a falsehood. Her smile adds in an almost endless spiral to the doubts he was already having. She smiles because she's already worked out the whacked math theorem and already knows the outcome that simply waited for her to turn round. She'd become accustomed to her effect upon people. If she were in a confessional mood she might tell him how she enjoyed the discomfort she caused, but then, this was not to be the night for any acts of contrition.

"Aren't you going to ask me to put my hands up or some such something," she almost purrs out the taunt that she's feeling, "yell freeze or police or something."

This is followed by her damned mocking smile though her eyes have not been brought up yet to look at him. He's not yet seen her face which adds to the unnerving effect as she knew it would. "Please do not disappoint me Mon capitaine." Now she casts a sidewards glance across to him but his gun stays aimed at center mass, and she's ever so slightly impressed.

"This is not a police matter anymore," he says.

"Personal then," she flatly states. "Good. I think it's better for it to be this way between us." She finishes saying as her grin fades at the corners of her mouth momentarily, which doesn't seem to suit the situation and makes him a touch more nervous.

"Did you think to make yourself a hero?" He asks her now returning the question she once put to him as he struggles to give his brain time to settle its internal trial. She likes this question even better than the ones previously asked. She finds it delicious and satisfying as she looks up to him for the first time. She casts her full gaze upon him. He tries to turn away from those damnded eyes of hers. Colorless eyes looking right through him that threatens a panic within him which she soaks up and he tries to tamp down.

"No hero I Mon capitaine," she says turned suddenly serious, "heroes die and hell is for them."

It has the effect she'd intended as the phrase seemingly pushed him to make a decision one way or the other. She did so without her caring really which way he was going to go with it mind you. She simply held a desperate desire on her part that he finally make a damn decision for fuck's sake.

embrace the night

An argument rages in his head, the din loud enough to raise the dead. He has her dead to rights, but he's conflicted about what to do with her. He knows logically and intellectually that he must end this whole charade. He understands that the least messiest course offered to conclude this is also the easiest and most logical path.

Simply put her down like she was a rabid mad dog. A mercy killing, pull the trigger of his pistol and put multiple bullets into her. Pour the whole damn clip into her until he was absolutely certain she'd never rise again. He's certainly free from any worry over any form of punishment or retribution. This whole episode is as close to tacitly sanctioned as one could get. But one thought always keeps bobbing up to give him pause as it has throughout this cheap serial. It's perhaps the single most important question any of us could and should ask ourselves. If he does what's been asked of him, is it the conclusion he himself wants, and is it what he wants to become of him.

He doesn't have the right questions to get the answers he'd previously thought he'd wanted from her let alone his own persistently nagging question. In all of their circling one another he suddenly realizes that he has not received any extra insight into her or her actions as he'd previously thought. Hell, he's pretty sure now he doesn't want any answers or anything else from her, finding himself long past the one time strong desire when he'd thought maybe he had.

He doesn't want to be troubled with her anymore or to know anything more about her. He's damned tired of the whole shitting mess and decides with a sudden clarity of a clean and sober unknown previously that he wants to be finally free from her and her riddles however that can best be achieved presently.

"I could shoot you," he says and neither one of them is sure if that sentence is a question or a statement.

She smiles that same damn wicked smile of hers and his anger grows. He resents this woman and her dead eyes, her wicked grins and long shadows. He's tired of the bullshit that comes with these invisible binds to her. Further resentment to find his person inexcusably linked in orbit around her, of being in relation to her, of the approximation and warped intimacy to her.

He looks down at his hand with the gun in it thinking how much he wants tonight to be freed from it all. There, in his hands. he believes is the vehicle that can take him there as his finger tightens on the trigger. He pulls the trigger taut, pressure increasing in micros, his concentration focusing on her as he slows his breath and aims. He hears her voice speak very clearly as she utters the same charge against him that he'd earlier attempted to press her with.

"Of course you could, killer," she taunts him further, "it's always been an option for us."

Still that same damn smile of hers flashes again as his gun drops to his side with his decision made. She's over to him in an instant, in a blink. She's upon him in an immeasurable split of time. She has him in her embrace, kissing him full upon the lips with a kiss unlike any kiss he's ever experienced before or ever will again. He feels every one of his troubles and pains rush away from him and into her. Not just todays, but from all throughout his life. It seems it would be a painful event, or at least one filled with rue and regret. A feeling, a grasp at things stolen or lost never to be recovered, but it's none of that. It's a flash of thought, of wonder at how the others who've fallen before her felt at this moment and finally explains the look in her eyes.

What he does feel, what there is, is an indescribable lifting of burden, a purge of all the weight of a life lived. He feels sins being lifted clean from his soul and a brief insight into the terribleness that is her.

She is a compilation of all the wrongs she's consumed. These wrongs she uses to fuel her power as the eater of evils. She offers this in a slim and brief glimpse before she's consumed this as well. He's caught in an almost overwhelming feeling of total happiness. An endless bliss and a sound; a very loud sound that feels very much like the crashing of a tsunami filling his head. He's lost safely within its surprisingly warm waters, with but one word left to lie upon his lips - rapture.

Darkest Night

final shots

She turns ruefully to look back over her shoulder at the detective still caught in the effects of her embrace. She very suddenly finds herself exhausted and bone-tired. Time to get some rest she thinks as she steps from the top of the warehouse and alights safely upon the pavement below. She pulls her thin short leather jacket to her fighting off an impossible cold that sits deep within her being. She stuffs her hands into the pockets as she steps off for the Quarter. Her heels clacking against the uneven pavement that's part brick and part concrete.

She wishes for a moment for some great ending. A fantastic shot like Orson Welles did with Dietrich. She'd dyed her hair black for him in that film and would do so only for him as she'd once famously said. Dietrich imparting a great line when asked about knowing a person and asking what did it matter before walking off down the road and leaving the dead where they lay. A fine example of anything at all that's been said or will about a person or being.

Damn but that's a little deep and probably inappropriate for the story told here. A little too heavy she thinks, given a value beyond the common currency. She thinks she'll stop for a pint at Molly's. Then maybe scare some tourists as it's now heading towards her favorite hour of darkest night, and then perhaps tomorrow she'll get some much needed rest.

ABOUT THE AUTHOR

Jack Kelly is a pseudonym, cause why be a writer and not use a pen name.